Grandpa's Suitcase of Stories

Grandpa's Suitcase of Stories

Stuti Agarwal

JUGGERNAUT BOOKS
C-I-128, First Floor, Sangam Vihar, Near Holi Chowk,
New Delhi 110080, India

First published by Juggernaut Books 2021

10 9 8 7 6 5 4 3

P-ISBN: 9789353451431
E-ISBN: 9789353451448

Typeset in Adobe Caslon Pro by R. Ajith Kumar, Noida

Printed at Thomson Press India Ltd

For Papa

Thank you for being my biggest cheerleader

Contents

Prologue

'Cuckoo Cuckoo! Cuckoo Cuckoo!'

'DING DING!'

The giant clock struck eight, and there was a sudden burst of activity in the Pais House.

Abir busied himself making a quilt tent on the bed and Megha jumped around the room picking up everything that would be needed – the cookie jar, torches and, most importantly, Grandpa's red suitcase.

Grandpa, meanwhile, was in the kitchen, pouring warm chocolate milk into a thermos, Dabbu jumping at his heels in excitement.

'Ready or not, here I come!' Grandpa yelled.

Giggling, the twins quickly turned off the

lights and sneaked into their tent, torches at the ready. It was Pyjama Story Time!

The schools in Dehradun were closed for winter vacation, which meant Megha and Abir would be at their grandpa's in Landour for two whole months. They looked forward to these holidays, and Grandpa's Pyjama Story Time was their favourite part of the day.

As a young man, Grandpa had been a botanist, travelling the country with his big red suitcase and discovering new plants.

The kids called it Grandpa's Magic Suitcase, because every time Grandpa stuck his head in it, he found a new story to tell.

Megha and Abir wondered what story Grandpa would pull out today. Would it be one of his own unbelievable adventures or a mystical tale?

'Let's see. What shall it be . . .' Grandpa said.

1

The Chicken Man

'A horror story?' Grandpa asked, sticking his head inside the suitcase.

'Woo . . . woof.'

'Grand . . . Grandpa, I think . . . horror . . . horror stories scare Dabbu,' stammered Abir.

'And you!' Grandpa chuckled.

'Tha . . . that's hardly true,' said Abir. 'I went to Pari . . . Pari Tibba with you today.'

'And ran back down in a minute, you chicken!' said Megha.

The four had spent the morning hiking up to Pari Tibba, a hilltop considered to be haunted. The plan was to have a picnic there, but as soon as they reached Abir scuttled back down with

Dabbu, certain that he had heard someone say 'boo' in his ear.

'Speaking of chicken,' Grandpa said, 'I've found it! The story of the Chicken Man.'

'The Chicken Man?' the kids screamed. 'YES YES YES!'

So Grandpa pulled his head out of the suitcase, put aside his spectacles and began.

In a small village, somewhere in the heart of Haryana, there once lived a man named Bahula. An ordinary man, all Bahula wanted was to eat good food, and plenty of it, but he did not wish to spend a rupee of his own on it.

Yes, Bahula was a miser. He would pile up his plate at someone else's feast, but if it came to spending his own money, he would fill himself up with a lot of water instead.

The villagers had even made up a poem in Miser Bahula's name!

Someone else's plate is Bahula's pick
To eat until his very last lick
But when his own money he must spend
He is not even his own best friend!

~

One day, as Bahula lay in the fields near his house, he began to feel very hungry. He had not eaten a morsel the whole day.

Just then, over the rumble of his stomach, he heard the clucking of a clutch of chickens.

The fields belonged to the richest landlord in the village, Seth Lal, and Bahula was certain the chickens were his too.

'Oh, what wouldn't I give for a leg of tandoori chicken right now,' he said with a sigh. 'I haven't had a piece of meat in months! What have I done to deserve this?'

Bahula grew hungrier with each word. And then a thought crossed his mind.

'But silly me! Here I am blaming the gods for not giving me meat when they have sent this family of chickens for me to pick one.'

Saying this, Bahula got up to chase the chickens and catch one for himself.

PUCK PUCK PUCK PUCKAAA!
PUCK PUCK PUCK
PUCK PUCKAAAA!

The chickens, sensing the threat, started running helter-skelter.

By the time Bahula caught the juiciest one, he was dripping buckets of sweat. But a satisfied man, Bahula stuffed the chicken under his shirt and marched back home.

He lost no time in cooking the chicken, and laughed to himself over the meal. 'What a clever plan! I wonder if Seth Lal will ever find out. I think I will repeat this for dinner tomorrow, and every day after that. I will not have to work another day in my life!'

~

Bahula went to bed happy and content. He slept soundly for hours, snoring away noisily over dreams of future feasts. In the middle of the night, however, he woke up feeling a nasty itch all over his body. It was unbearable, but with no oil for his lamp, he couldn't see what was causing it and had to wait till morning to find out.

As soon as he saw the first rays of the sun, Bahula stepped out of the house.

'What on earth!' he screamed.

There were red spots all over his body, and little chicken feathers were sprouting from under them.

By the afternoon the chicken feathers had covered him from head to toe, sparing only his face and hands. He even had a chicken feather mohawk!

'NOOOOOOOOOOOOOOO,' he cried, and began plucking the feathers out in handfuls.

OUCH! OUCH! OUCH! OUCH!

OUCH OUCH! OUCH OUCH!

He kept plucking them, but the feathers came back thicker and bigger.

'The gods have tricked me!' he wailed. 'They made me steal the chicken, and now they are punishing me for it by turning me into one!'

Bahula sobbed for the rest of the day. Finally, tired of the useless plucking and pain, he went to bed.

~

That night, after Bahula fell into an uneasy sleep, Pari the fairy came to visit him in his dreams.

'Oh, my poor Bahula,' Pari said. 'You've landed yourself in such trouble. Why must you be so lazy when everyone else works? Why not earn food for yourself?'

'You're right, P . . . PUCK PUCK . . . Pari,' cried Bahula, who was turning more and more into a chicken. 'But how am I to work with all these feathers?'

Pari laughed. 'You should see them as a blessing! You will not need any clothes this winter. Why complain?'

But when Bahula wouldn't stop crying, Pari softened a little. 'Are you truly sorry for years of laziness and wicked deeds?'

Bahula would have thought longer, but with the feathers poking him harder each minute, he screamed, 'YES . . . PUCK . . . YES! I will do . . . PUCK . . . anything you say. PUCK . . . just free me . . . PUCK . . . of these feathers.'

'If only. I cannot free you of them. You must do

it yourself. What you need is a good scolding. Go to Seth Lal and get him to scold you. The harder he scolds, the sooner your feathers will fall out.'

~

Bahula woke up from the dream a happy and determined man. He would go to Seth Lal and confess his crime. That way he would get a scolding and be feather-free. He had truly led a lazy life, and he would not be lazy another day.

'I will . . . PUCK . . . make . . . PUCK . . . a good man of myself, I . . . PUCK . . . really will.'

And so he put on a set of clean clothes, covered his mohawk with a hat and took out some money from his hiding place under the mattress to pay Seth Lal before setting out.

He was halfway to Seth Lal's when he felt his pocket and was overcome by a horrible feeling. He hated parting with his money. He was a miser after all.

'Hey, hadn't Pari . . . PUCK . . . said that I only had . . . PUCK PUCK . . . to listen to a good scolding? She . . . PUCK . . . never . . . PUCK . . . said anything about confessing to . . . PUCK . . . stealing,' he thought to himself slyly. 'That's right! All I need to . . . PUCK . . . do is get him to scold someone and hear it. Why don't I tell him . . . PUCK . . . Tripathi stole his chicken? That should do it. It will save me . . . PUCK PUCK . . . from spending my money and teach the rotten Tripathi a . . . PUCK . . . lesson for making fun of me. Besides, who's to say Seth . . . PUCK . . . Lal . . . PUCK . . . won't hand me over to the police? Yes, this will be best.'

The longer Bahula talked to himself, the more convinced he became of his plan. By the time he reached Seth Lal's, he was confident this was the only way.

~

Now Seth Lal was a generous man, adored by the whole village. When he heard Bahula had come to meet him, he invited the man in for tea and snacks.

'Well, what is it that worries you, dear Bahula?'

'I have something . . . PUCK . . . important to tell . . . PUCK . . . you about your chickens, Sethji,' said Bahula, piling up his plate with samosas and matthis.

'My chickens?'

'That's a good . . . PUCK . . . clutch of . . . CRUNCH . . . chickens you have there.'

'Ah yes, a fine clutch indeed.'

'How many . . . PUCK . . . are there?'

'Fifteen.'

'PUCK . . . did you count . . . CRUNCH . . . them yesterday?'

'I did. There was one missing. But a chicken is hardly of any importance. Why do you ask?'

'But surely . . . PUCK . . . PUCK . . . you want to know . . . PUCK . . . how you lost one.'

'A hawk most likely.'

'No . . . CRUNCH. It was . . . PUCK . . . Tri . . . PUCK . . . pathi.'

'What? You think Tripathi stole my chicken?'

'Exactly . . . PUCK! You understand now.'

'Well, that's too bad. I am sorry the old man is going through a tough time. He is a hard-working man and should be paid better. If only he had asked, I would have given him a chicken.'

Bahula waited for Seth Lal to get angry, but no such thing happened. Instead, Seth Lal only became more sorry for Tripathi.

'Are you sure . . . PUCK . . . you don't want to . . . PUCK CRUNCH . . . scold him?' Bahula pressed. 'A good . . . PUCK . . . beating maybe?'

'For a measly chicken? Never.'

Meanwhile, the feathers on Bahula were

becoming more and more painful. Afraid of having to live with them for another minute, he threw himself at Seth Lal's feet.

'Sethji! I am a . . . PUCK . . . very bad . . . . PUCK . . . man. I might as well . . . PUCK . . . give up . . . PUCK PUCK . . . I . . . PUCK . . . stole your . . . PUCK . . . chicken.'

'I know,' said Seth Lal calmly. I saw you carrying the chicken under your shirt, but why are you confessing to me now?'

Bahula quickly narrated what had happened and begged Seth Lal to scold him for his crime.

Seth Lal broke into a loud laugh. 'HAHAHAHA HAHAHA HEHE HEHE. CHICKEN FEATHERS! WHAT A WONDERFUL TALE! HAHAHAHAHAHA.'

Bahula got more miserable by the second, 'Scold . . . PUCK . . . me, I beg you. SCOLD . . .

PUCK PUCK . . . ME!'

But Seth Lal went on laughing. 'Show me your feathers first and then we'll talk about a scolding.'

Bahula obeyed.

'Well, now that's something. They must keep you very warm.' Seth Lal laughed. 'And you hate to work. These will save you from dressing up in the morning!'

'I CAN BARELY STAND THE . . . PUCK . . . PAIN. AND . . . AND . . . PUCK . . . AND THEY ITCH ALL OVER. AND I'M CLUCKING . . . PUCK,' Bahula screamed.

'Be calm, dear Bahula. I am not used to getting angry. You must give me time to think of a good scolding.'

By now Bahula was in so much pain that he began banging his head against Seth Lal's legs, 'SCOLD ME! SCOLD . . . PUCK . . . ME!'

Seth Lal, too, had had enough. Besides, he was getting mighty poked by Bahula's feather mohawk. He got up and shouted, 'YOU LAZY MAN! YOU GOOD-FOR-NOTHING COCKROACH! I WISH NOTHING MORE THAN GETTING RID OF YOU AND YOUR CHICKEN FEATHERS!'

For a man who never got angry, this was a very serious scolding. No sooner had the first words come out of his mouth than the feathers began falling off. By the time Seth Lal was done yelling, all the feathers were on the floor.

Free from the pain, Bahula jumped up, collected all the feathers and handed them to Seth Lal.

'Thank you so much for your kindness, Sethji. You have freed me from my pain and for that

I present you with these feathers along with the full payment for the chicken I stole. I have learnt my lesson. From this day on, I shall be an honest man. Goodbye and many thanks again.'

With that, Bahula left Seth Lal's house and became a wise, hard-working man.

'I'll never steal laddoos from the cupboard again!' cried out Abir.

'You're right, Abir, because eating too many laddoos will turn you into one!' Grandpa laughed.

2

The Boy Who Opened the Door

Megha and Abir had had a long day running around the town, helping their neighbour, Mrs Tomar, put up posters to find her missing pet parakeet.

'Nimbu has run away once again,' announced Megha, taking off her coat and slumping into the kitchen chair.

It was the third time in the last two weeks. The parakeet had really mastered the art of cracking the window open.

'Oho. She just likes to go to peck at the pine trees in the winters,' said Grandpa. 'I should go tell Mrs Tomar not to worry.'

'And not waste all that paper. Nimbu is always back home in a day or two!' Abir piped in.

'You know, back when I was travelling, I helped find a missing boy once,' Grandpa said, handing over glasses of his special cola float to the tired kids.

Megha and Abir jumped up in excitement.

'Oh, do tell us the story, Grandpa!'

'Mrs Tomar gave us a lot of cookies to eat. Can't we skip dinner today and get to story time?'

'Please, Grandpa! Please please please!'

'Okay. Hop into your PJs,' Grandpa said.

It was a very cold winter in Himachal Pradesh. Out of work, Budhu's parents were forced to leave for the city to earn a living, and little Budhu was sent to his dadi who lived in the forest.

Now every morning Budhu's dadi would make her way to the town to sell her home-made pickles. With Budhu at home, she woke up early to make him a bowl of her special egg rice and said to him, 'Budhu darling, here is your lunch. Have it on time, and remember, stay indoors and do not open the door for anyone but me.'

'Yes, Dadi,' Budhu said before rushing back to his video game.

Dadi had only been gone ten minutes when Gilheri, the neighbourhood fox, smelt the egg rice and came knocking. Knock knock!

'Oh Budhu!' she called. 'Open the door!'

'No, I mustn't open the door for anyone but Dadi,' replied Budhu.

But the sly old fox kept knocking, louder and louder.

KNOCK KNOCK KNOCK KNOCK KNOCK!!

'But Budhu, you know me, I'm no stranger!'

KNOCK KNOCK, KNOCK KNOCK KNOCK!!

'Listen Budhu,' she called out, 'if you open the door, I'll give you a ride on my long tail.'

On hearing this, Budhu put down his video game and thought to himself, 'Wouldn't that be fun! A ride on Gilheri's bushy tail.'

So little Budhu forgot what Dadi had told him and opened the door, and in dashed cunning Gilheri. She went straight to the bowl of egg rice on the table and gobbled it up to the last grain.

Budhu had nothing left to eat for lunch.

When Dadi returned in the evening, she found Budhu sitting in the corner, crying.

'Why are crying my child?' she asked.

'I'm hungry,' Budhu wailed.

'Budhu, did you open the door and let someone in?' Dadi asked suspiciously.

'Umm . . . yes . . . Gilheri. And she ate all my lunch!'

'Now you see what happens when you open the door. You must remember never to open the door for anyone but me.'

~

The next morning Dadi made some mutton cutlets. Before leaving the house she called out to Budhu from the door, 'I've left you some mutton cutlets, Budhu. Eat them soon and remember not to open the door for anyone while I'm gone.'

Gilheri, who was scampering nearby, smelt the delicious mutton cutlets, and no sooner had Dadi left than she came knocking once again.

KNOCK KNOCK!

'Dear friend, it's me – Gilheri. Open the door!'

'Go away, I shall not open the door for you,' screamed Budhu.

KNOCK KNOCK, KNOCK KNOCK KNOCK! KNOCK KNOCK, KNOCK KNOCK KNOCK!!

'Come now, please open the door,' Gilheri begged. 'You know me, and if you open the door I will give you a ride on my soft tail. Truly I will!'

Budhu put aside his playing cards and thought to himself, 'Maybe this time she really will give me a ride on her tail.'

So he opened the door.

Oh, what a mistake.

ZOOP — ZAP — ZIP

Before Budhu knew it, Gilheri had zooped in, zapped the mutton cutlets down her throat and zipped out.

At lunchtime, Budhu was left hungry again.

When Dadi came home to a sobbing Budhu, she knew he had opened the door a second time.

'It was Gilheri and she promised me a ride on her tail!' he cried.

'Budhu, you bad boy. How many times have I told you that you mustn't open the door? I shall punish you with porridge for the rest of the summer if you do it again,' she yelled.

~

To cheer up the little boy, Dadi woke up super early the next day and made some of Budhu's favourite spicy chicken stew.

The stew really did cheer Budhu up in an instant and he began eating it as soon as Dadi left for the day.

It smelt scrumpdelicious! And, sure enough, Gilheri smelt it too.

'Oh Budhu! Let me in!' she sang.

But Budhu refused to open the door. He sat himself by the window where Gilheri could see him and slurped on the stew.

Now that would have only angered the wily Gilheri, but she calmly called out to Budhu, 'My dear Budhu, please open the door. This time I promise I'll give you a ride on my strong tail. Truly I will, I really will.

Gilheri begged and begged and begged until finally Budhu opened the door.

Gilheri jumped into the room and dived towards the bowl.

SLURP!

And nothing. The bowl was empty.

'Oh, I'm sorry, did you want some of the stew? I've finished it all,' Budhu said, smiling.

Now this should have surely angered Gilheri, but the devious fox said sweetly, 'That's all right. Why don't you get on my tail and I'll give you a ride?'

So Budhu, excited that his plan had worked, climbed on to Gilheri's tail.

WHOOSH —

— WHISH —

— WOOP

Gilheri blazed through the room, out of the hut, across the forest and into her hole, dropping off Budhu with her two little ones who teased and bit him blue. Boy, was Budhu sorry he hadn't listened to Dadi yet again.

When Dadi came back home, she found the door wide open and Budhu missing. She looked and looked, asked everyone she met, but she could not find the little boy. So poor Dadi went back home and cried all night and day.

~

A week later, I was wandering through the forest looking for new plants when I crossed Dadi's house.

'I've found gooey. I've found sweet. I've found long and short and hard and soft and muddy and sharp and shiny. I've found plants of all kinds,' I was singing to myself looking at all the new plants I'd discovered.

The call reminded Dadi of Budhu's songs and she came out to greet me. 'Sir, can you please not sing any more. Your song makes me cry.'

'Why does it make you cry?' I asked.

'It reminds me of my little Budhu who was stolen from me just a few days ago,' she wept.

'Oh no!' I said. 'I'll tell you what I'll do. I will go around finding my plants and keep an eye out for the little boy.'

'Ble . . . bless . . . bless you, sir,' Dadi stammered.

~

I went around for days but there was no sign of the boy.

As I was crossing the forest on my way back to Dadi's house to give her the bad news, I thought I heard a boy crying. I decided to follow the sobs, and they brought me to a fox's hole.

'Of course, it must be Gilheri!' I thought to

myself. 'The wicked fox must have stolen the boy just like she stole my equipment the other day.'

I quickly made up a song and began to sing:

There's one old fox
With two little ones
Another that she stole
Makes all of four.

Gilheri heard the song and, afraid of getting caught, sent her oldest child to shoo me away, saying, 'Here, son. Give the man a rupee and tell him to go away.'

The little fox climbed up the hole and out of it. 'My mother has requested you to take this rupee and not come back.'

As I reached for the rupee, I caught the little fox and stuffed him in a sack. Then I continued my song:

There is one old fox
With one little one
Another one she stole
Makes all of three.

Getting even more worried, Gilheri sent her second child with a rupee to ask me to stop.

I added the second fox to my sack and continued singing:

There is one old fox
And no little one
Another that she stole
Makes two of all.

Left with no more young foxes, Gilheri decided she had to come out herself to shoo me away, but before she knew it, I jumped at her from behind the tree and stuffed her into the sack.

Then I stepped closer to the hole and called out, 'Budhu, Budhu, come out now!'

With no one left to beat him up, Budhu scuttled out of the hole, crying.

'Un . . . Uncle. I want to . . . I want to go home to m . . . my dadi. Please take me back to her.'

'Of course, Budhu. Don't worry, but first I must teach these naughty foxes a lesson.'

And with that I broke a branch from a tree and began beating the foxes in the sack.

'OUCH!'

'OUCH!'

'OUCH!'

'AAAAAAAAAAOOOOO OOOOOOOOOO!'

'OOOOOOOOOOOOOOO WWWWWWWWWWWWWW WWWWWW!'

I stopped when they promised never to trouble anyone again. Then I held the sack above my head and threw it far far away.

'WOOOOOOOOOOOOO
OOOOOOOOOOOOOOOOOOOO
OOOOOOOOOOOOOoooooooooo!'

You could hear the two tiny foxes enjoying their flight.

'WOOOOOOOOOOOOO
OOOOOOOOOOOOOoooooooooo!'

Budhu's dadi was delighted to have her grandson back and thanked me with a big meal of egg rice, mutton cutlets and spicy chicken stew. The three of us ate heartily, and Budhu never opened the door for a stranger again.

'You really beat the foxes?' Abir asked in disbelief.

'Of course!' said Grandpa. 'Your grandpa could handle a wolf in the old days!'

The kids could hardly believe their grandpa, but they loved him and his stories too much to argue.

'All that talk about food has made me hungry,' said Megha.

'I should have never let you kids skip dinner!' said Grandpa, shaking his head.

'Midnight feast!' cried Abir.

3

The Boy Who Liked to Sew

Grandpa and Megha were trying their best to cheer Abir up. Earlier in the morning he had fallen off a slide and scraped both his knees and palms. Needless to say, there was a lot of crying.

Abir was sad all day, even with the three of them eating his favourite meal of pizza for lunch as they watched *Ratatouille*, his favourite movie.

The evening looked up with only a few sniffles here and there as the three went out to town for ice cream shakes and a cycle ride around Mall Road.

By Pyjama Story Time, Megha and Grandpa were sure they would finally get Abir to smile.

'I can see the story of a brave boy,' said Grandpa, sticking his head inside the suitcase.

'A brave boy!' exclaimed Megha, glancing over at Abir.

'Fine,' Abir sulked.

'Get ready for some time travel, kids. This is the story of Pankaj Gupta.'

'Who's Pankaj Gupta, Grandpa?'

'He's one of the biggest fashion designers in the world, Megha!'

'And where do we travel to?' asked Abir, sitting up.

'We travel back twenty-five years to Jodhpur, when Pankaj was a little boy, as old as you two.'

Pankaj was eight when his two sisters got their first embroidery hoops and handkerchiefs. They were nine and eleven.

He sat beside them, fascinated, watching his mother teach them how to cross-stitch their names in green and red.

'I want to learn embroidery, too!' Pankaj declared.

'Boys don't embroider. Now don't disturb your sisters and go out to play with your friends,' she shouted. Pankaj's mother was a single parent and worked at a small boutique as an embroiderer. The five of them – the three children, their nani and their mother – lived in a small house in Jodhpur with no help. With the embroidery lessons, Pankaj's mother was hoping the daughters would soon be able to lend her a hand.

That night, once everyone was asleep, Pankaj snuck out of bed, stole a hoop and some thread and cross-stitched his name on to the folded end of a curtain in the unused guest room.

'No one will see this,' he thought.

Pankaj was certain his cross-stitch was neater than his sisters'!

From that day on, every time his sisters sat down to embroider, Pankaj would watch until his mother shooed him off to play.

'I do not want to see you around!' she would yell. 'The next time I see you here, you will not be allowed any time to play at all.'

Now Pankaj didn't really enjoy outdoor games, so every evening during playtime he began running off to the artists' colony nearby to watch zari embroidery being done. And every night, using his sisters' embroidery material, he practised what he saw there.

~

For months Pankaj practised on the curtains in the guest room without anyone finding out. He filled them with cross-stitched roses and bees, leaves in all colours and peacocks made of French knots. But someone had to find out some day, right?

Diwali was around the corner and the guest room was to be cleaned for Pankaj's mama who was coming to visit. Pankaj's heart pounded as he watched his nani and mother take trips to the room. He knew the curtains would come off soon. How could he have forgotten!

'PANKU PANKU!' he heard Nani scream.

His cover was blown.

'Yes . . . yes, Nani,' Pankaj stammered, standing at the door.

'Come in here.'

She was sitting on the bed, the curtains in her hand.

'I know you did this.'

He looked at her but said nothing.

She stayed silent for a few minutes and then said, 'I will take care of these. You will practise on my saris from now on.'

With that she left the room.

No one ever found out about the curtains. They remained Pankaj and Nani's secret.

Diwali was as great as the year before and the year before that and the year before that. Pankaj loved Mama and looked forward to his visits. It was also the only time they got real gifts. That year Pankaj got a race car and his sisters a make-your-own-stuffed-animals kit and a table weaving loom.

~

Once Mama left, Pankaj went back to his embroidery practice. Every night he would sneak out of bed and into Nani's room, where she would give him a sari to practise on. He even completed the crochet handkerchiefs and patchwork bed sheets that Nani was making for his sisters' weddings.

He was very happy.

Then came the day when the final report card arrived at the house.

Pankaj could hear his mother from a street away as he walked back home from school.

'THAT BRAT. LET HIM GET HOME, I'LL SET HIM RIGHT.'

'ALL RED! ALL. RED.'

'WHO'S EVER FAILED THE SECOND GRADE?'

'A THRASHING! THAT'S WHAT HE NEEDS.'

'Stay calm, stay calm,' he heard Nani say as he crept into the house.

He quickly ran in and hid behind her.

'That's not going to make a difference at all. Come out right this minute.'

'Na . . . Nani,' Pankaj whimpered, clinging to her sari.

'Beta, we have to speak to him calmly; beating

him will not help.'

'Mummy, you please stay out of this. Pankaj Gupta, you better come out here before I finish counting to five, or else . . .'

'ONE.'

'TWO.'

'THREE'

'DO I HAVE TO GO ON OR HAVE YOU FORGOTTEN YOUR COUNTING TOO, PANKAJ?'

Of course, he had to come out from behind Nani. He had never seen his mother this mad and didn't want to know what 'or else' meant. But boy, was she right about the thrashing.

It was the thrashing of a lifetime.

~

From that day on, Pankaj's mother kept a close eye on him. While his sisters got to embroider after homework hour, he sat for extra classes.

It was worse than playing cricket with the boys!

His nani, too, stopped the embroidery lessons.

'Not now, Panku. You have to concentrate on your studies.'

'But I don't want to study science and maths! I don't like studying at all!'

'You must, Panku. Every good boy must study.'

There was no getting out of it. For the next six months Pankaj did nothing but study.

~

When the half-yearly report came, Pankaj had passed in all the subjects. His grades were not great, but they were an improvement from the previous year. His mother didn't say anything. However, she did make him some of her special gulab jamun curry that day.

The rules could now be relaxed.

There was still no play hour, but Pankaj managed to convince Nani to let him resume embroidery practice.

'Please Naan-bread,' he begged. 'My grades are better and I am still studying through playtime.'

'I don't know, Panku. Your mummy will not be happy if she finds out.'

'But my grades were bad only because I wasn't studying earlier, and I'm studying all day now! Pleaseeeeeeeeeeeee, Nani!'

'Panku . . . I don't . . .'

'I'll be careful, Nani, promise!'

Finally, she agreed, and Pankaj went back to his nightly embroidery practice. Every day he would wait for everyone to be asleep before creeping to Nani's room. She would light a lamp and place it in the cupboard, and Pankaj would sit inside, embroidering for hours.

~

Perhaps it was because he was out of practice or all the studying that was tiring him, but on one of these nights Pankaj woke up in the cupboard, the blouse he was embroidering beads on still in his lap.

He took a moment before crawling out. The daylight was blinding. Nani must be out at the temple for her morning puja, he thought. He slowly opened the door of the room, hoping to tiptoe his way across the dining hall and to his room without bumping into his mother.

There was absolute silence, and he felt certain no one else was awake yet.

He was wrong.

He had only made it halfway across the dining hall when his gaze went to the sofa. And there she sat – Mummy, with Nani and his sisters next to her.

Mummy said nothing. They stared at each other for some time. Pankaj decided it would be best to go to her before she called him.

He was wrong again. Not about going to the sofa, but about his last beating being the thrashing of a lifetime.

This was the thrashing of a lifetime.

Mummy said nothing throughout. She pulled Pankaj up by his ear and propped him up on the dining table. Pankaj instinctively knew that he had to take the chicken pose – his hands going around his legs and clutching his ears. And then the thrashing began.

'AAAAAAAAAAAAAAAHHHHHHHH HHHHHHHHHHHHHHHHHHHHHHH HHH!'

'MUMMAAAAEEEEE.'

'MUMMY NAHI, PLEASE!'

'Please, Mummy. Sorry.'

'AAH HUH HUH UH HUH!'

'He'll get hurt, beta.'

'The neighbours will hear, beta,' Nani intervened a few times, but Pankaj's mother did not stop and Pankaj continued to scry (scream+cry).

His sisters, meanwhile, sat on the sofa, practising how to make a flower using knot-stitch. He later told them their flowers were very shoddy. Usually they would have bullied him about it, but that day they felt too sorry for him to do anything.

~

After a few days of complete silence and only karela and tinda to eat, Mama came to visit. It was an untimely visit. Pankaj was surprised, and so were Nani and his sisters.

That evening Mummy finally spoke, only to tell everyone of a decision she had made.

'Pankaj will be moving to Lucknow with his mama.'

'What?' screamed Nani.

'What?' screamed his sisters.

'No!' screamed Pankaj.

'Panku, it will be okay,' said Mama calmly. 'You will go to school there and I will take care of you.'

'But Nani is here, and my friends are here.'

'You have no friends; you don't even play with them,' scoffed his mother.

'He's your son, beta,' Nani reasoned. 'You can't send him away.'

'I have had enough of this boy. No more!'

'I will not leave. I am studying now and my grades are better. All I did was embroider, and you can't send me away for that!' Pankaj cried.

'Boys don't embroider! And no one asked you if you want to go. You will leave with Mama in two days.'

~

On the third day, Pankaj left with Mama over tearful goodbyes with Nani and his sisters. His mother did not speak a word.

Pankaj had a rough first week at the new school.

Mama was kind to him. He made his favourite food and helped him with schoolwork, but Pankaj missed Nani and his sisters.

'Panku, you have a great day at school today,' Mama said as they sat at the table for a breakfast of omelettes and milk one day. 'I will take you out for some pizza for dinner!'

'Okay, Mama.'

'Panku?'

'Yes?'

'How about we also go shopping for some new toys?'

'Do you need new toys, Mama?'

'Uh . . . no.'

'Can we leave for school now?'

'Yes, yes, let's,' said Mama.

~

That night, as they ate pizza, Mama fished out a bag from under the table and handed it to Pankaj.

'What is this, Mama?'

'You'll find out when you open it.'

Pankaj carefully slipped his hand into the bag and pulled out a big box.

'The weaving loom! How did you . . .'

'Keep looking.'

Pankaj looked in the bag again.

'Threads and needles!'

'Twenty different colours.' Mama smiled. 'Keep going.'

'Hoops of so many sizes!'

'An embroidery guide!'

'A crochet kit!'

'There's one last thing.'

Two of Nani's favourite saris.

Pankaj started to cry. He missed her so much.

'Panku,' Mama spoke calmly, 'Nani showed me your embroidery work when I was in Jodhpur. You have a gift, and I promised her that I would help you with it. But your mother wants you to study, and she's not wrong. You need to study too, only then can you grow up to go to college and become a designer.'

'A . . . a de-designer?'

'Isn't that what you want to be?'

'Perhaps. I would like to make clothes.'

'Well, you must study to be successful even at making clothes. Think about it this way: maths will help you with measurements, which you will need to make clothes; history will help you in learning about old styles and crafts; chemistry will teach you about colours and dyes. Every subject will teach you something.'

'I never thought of it that way,' Pankaj said, smiling.

'I will help you become a designer if you promise to study and do well. I'll even find you a tutor who can teach you tailoring.'

'Thank you, Mama,' Pankaj screamed, hugging him tightly.

~

Pankaj began to study hard. He hurried back from school every day and went to a nearby tailor for classes. In the evening, he finished all his schoolwork before dinner and got a good night's sleep.

On the weekends, Mama and he went out for outings and pizzas.

When his mother, sisters and nani visited

them in the summers, the schoolteachers gave the boy a great report.

Pankaj showed Nani the saris that he had embroidered with birds and trees, exchanged them with three new ones to practise on and gave his sisters the crochet dresses he had made for them.

He even gave his mother a cross-stitched bag. The two were no longer mad at each other.

Pankaj finished school in Lucknow and applied to a design college. The rest of the story is as you know it.

'I know what I want to be!' said Abir. 'I want to be a chef and make the best pizzas in the world!'

'I think I will be a journalist like Mummy,' Megha added.

'I'm sure you'll both make me proud,' said Grandpa, 'and if nothing else, you'll be paid well as professional missing poster stickers!'

The three of them laughed, Abir the loudest.

4

How the Emu Lost Its Wings and the Bustard Its Children

'Rules at the Nanda Devi National Park,' Megha read as they waited for their turn at the safari. Grandpa had brought the kids to Chamoli for the weekend.

1. Do not feed the animals
2. Do not touch any plants
3. Do not litter
4. Do not get out of the vehicle
5. Do not wear bright colours
6. Do not break the silence, and most importantly–

'I want binoculars like him!' a kid in the line cried, pointing at the one tangled around Abir's neck.

'I want one now!' he wailed.

'What a spoilt child,' muttered an aunty standing right behind him.

'You know, someone once told me about a bird just like that boy,' said Grandpa. 'Of course, she didn't meet a good end, and I sure hope that doesn't happen with him.'

'All right! Story time in the jungle!' Abir shouted.

Before they knew it, all the children, and a few adults, had gathered around Grandpa to listen in.

Emu, the largest bird in the Kutch desert, was accepted as the king by all birds. The bustard, being next in line, was always jealous of the emu.

The bustard mother, Googly, was especially

jealous of the emu mother, Nema, wishing she had Nema's big wings and high flight.

She would often sit and think of ways to put an end to the rule of the emus.

'I must get rid of their wings,' thought Googly one day.

But to challenge Nema to a fight would be foolish. Everyone knew a bustard didn't stand a chance in front of an emu. Googly would have to defeat her with trickery.

She came up with a plan and waited patiently for the right day to carry it out.

~

After a few weeks, when Googly saw Nema coming down from a long flight, she squatted close to her and tucked her wings in to make it look like she had none. It was time to set the plan in motion.

Googly chatted with Nema about the desert,

its rising heat and the drying water. Then, when Nema was about to leave, she said, 'You know, I think the desert will soon crown a bustard as the bird king.'

'Why do you think so?'

'Well, every bird flies. When they see that bustards can do without wings, they will know we are the mightiest birds in the desert.'

'But you have wings,' said Nema.

'No, I have no wings.' And indeed, Googly had tucked in her wings so well that her words seemed true. 'Perhaps you should cut yours off to remain the bird king.'

Nema went back home worried. She spoke to her husband, who was the reigning bird king, and he was just as worried.

'We can't have that at all,' he said. 'The bustards will prove to be bullies.'

Finally, they decided that they must both do away with their wings.

As soon as the operation was over, Nema lost no time in going to Googly to inform her of what they had done. She swiftly ran down to the plain where they had last met. Seeing Googly still squatting there, she said, 'See, I have followed your example and become a more powerful bird. I have cut off my wings and now have none.'

'HA HA HA!' Googly laughed, jumping up and opening her wings as she danced around Nema. 'I have fooled you! You can hardly be kings when you are so easily fooled. HA HA HA!'

Nema ran towards Googly in anger, but she flew away, and wingless, Nema could not follow her.

~

Nema dragged herself back home, crying over how easily she had been tricked. With her husband, she vowed to take revenge. But how? Nema thought for days, and once she had a plan, she prepared to implement it at once.

With the help of her husband, she hid all their children but two under a big saltbush. Then she walked over to Googly's plain with her two little emus.

Nema spoke to Googly in a friendly manner, talking about the increasing garbage in the desert. When Googly was gathering her children to leave, Nema said, 'Feeding twelve little ones must be very difficult. There is not enough food to turn them into big birds. You should be like us and have only two.'

With that, Nema walked away, leaving behind a worried Googly.

There was no doubt that the young emus were much bigger than the young bustards. Googly wondered if it was indeed because of

the limited food and their large numbers that they were smaller.

'It will be great to grow as big as the emus,' Googly said to herself.

She looked over at Nema's two children hopping behind their mother and her blood boiled with envy at how much bigger the young emus were than any of her children. She would not have it. She would rather get rid of her children.

'The emu will not be the bird king of the desert. The bustards will replace the emus. My children will grow to be as big as them and shall keep their wings and fly.'

Straight away, Googly got rid of all her young ones but two and went to where Nema was feeding her children.

Nema noticed Googly coming with only two young bustards and called out to her, 'Where are all your young ones?'

'I have gotten rid of them. Now I have only two. These two will have plenty to eat and will grow as big as your young ones.'

'You greedy mother!' Nema screamed in shock. 'You are a cruel mother to kill your children. Why, I have twelve children and I find enough food to feed them all. I would not kill them for anything, not even my wings. There is plenty for all. Look at the saltbush covered with berries to feed my whole family. See how the grasshoppers jump around the bush so we can fill ourselves on them.'

'But you have only two children.'

'I have twelve.'

Saying this, Nema ran off to the saltbush to gather all her little ones. Soon Googly saw Nema return, her neck stretched forward, her head thrown back in pride and her feathers swinging as she danced. With her were twelve soft, striped, furry little ones.

When Nema reached Googly, she stopped booing and said to her, 'Here are my twelve. And while you think about the evil you have caused, let me tell you the fate of bustards forever. We have lost our wings because of your dishonesty, and now for evermore you will have only two young ones. We are equal now. You have your wings and I my children.'

And ever since, emus have no wings and bustards lay only two eggs in a season.

'Of course, that's just a folk tale,' said Grandpa, looking at the shocked faces of the parents around him. 'But it sure is a good lesson on the ill effects of jealousy and wanting everything, isn't it?' he added, a twinkle in his eye as he looked at the boy who had been demanding the binoculars.

5

The Three Brothers

For a few days now, Grandpa had had an additional pair of ears at Pyjama Story Time. Abir's friend Kartik was visiting.

'Grandpa, can you see another animal story in there?' Kartik asked.

'Looking, darling.'

'You see, Kartik and I really like stories of the jungle,' seconded Abir. 'And I'm sure Dabbu would like an animal story too.'

'This is the hundredth jungle story in a row, Abir. I want a royal story,' said Megha.

'But Kartik is leaving in a day and we want–'

'Now don't fight, I think I may have found a story that will please all of you.'

In a forest near Ujjain, there once lived a young widow and her three sons. With their father long gone, the family was poor and relied on the forest for a living.

Every few months, the boys would go hunting deep into the forest. The youngest boy, a lot smaller and weaker than the other two, was always left behind.

And so, all day long he would gather wood, carry water from the stream and tend to the vegetable garden with his mother.

Even when his brothers were home, they would shoo him away.

'You're always doing foolish things. You're a burden to have around,' they'd say.

His brothers called him Shunya and all the neighbours teased him for having only half a brain.

His mother was the only one who was kind to the boy. 'They may laugh at you and call you a fool now, but you will be wiser than all of them. I was told so by a forest fairy at the time of your birth,' she always said.

~

A kind king, aided by his virtuous daughter, ruled the forest and the town of Ujjain. The princess had many suitors, but her father disapproved of them all.

One day, tired of having to send suitors away, he made an announcement in the town. 'The princess is still young. When it is time for her to get married, she will only marry a hard-working man who makes a great fortune from hunting.'

The two older brothers heard the news and

decided that one of them must win the princess.

'This is our chance to work hard and turn our fortune around,' they said.

It was autumn and the hunter's moon was upon them. They prepared to set out on a great hunting expedition.

'I want to come along!' said Shunya.

'Much help that will be.' The two brothers laughed. 'He will only bring us bad luck.'

But their mother commanded them to take their little brother along, and they had to obey.

So the three brothers set out for the north forest that was dense with animals, the two big brothers teasing the little one all the way.

~

A few weeks passed. The two brothers had great success and hunted many animals – deer, rabbits, boars and beavers. They came home with abundant quantities of dried meat and skins.

'This will prove our skill as hunters to the king, and if we do just as well next year when the hunter's moon shows up again, surely one of us will win his daughter's hand,' they told their mother.

'Look what I got, Mother,' their little brother added.

Shunya put out his hand and there it was – an earthworm as thick as his finger, wrapped all the way up his arm. It was the biggest earthworm he had ever seen! He thought of it as such a great discovery that he spent all his days in the hunt watching the earthworm and doing little else.

'We told you Shunya was a fool!' the brothers sniggered. 'Now he has proven it.'

They went around telling everyone of Shunya's great hunt of the earthworm and before long the town was laughing at the little boy again.

But his mother smiled and said, 'One day he will surprise everyone.'

~

Shunya made a tiny pen for the earthworm in the vegetable garden and fed it every few hours. One day a large duck came waddling by, stuck her bill over the fence and swallowed the earthworm.

Shunya was very angry and took the duck to the man who owned it. 'Your duck ate my worm. I want my worm back.'

The man offered to pay the price for the worm but Shunya insisted, 'I don't want your money. I want my worm.'

'But your worm is gone forever. My duck ate it.'

'It is not gone. It is in the duck's stomach. So I must have the duck.'

'There is no use arguing with a fool,' thought the man and gave Shunya his duck.

~

Shunya kept the duck in the pen he had built for his earthworm and tied a heavy stone to its foot so it wouldn't fly away.

He was quite happy. 'Now I have both my worm and the duck,' he thought.

He would feed and talk to the duck every few hours.

Then, one day, a fox came looking for food. He saw the fat duck with a stone tied to its foot and said, 'What luck! This duck shall be my meal for the day.'

The duck quacked as loudly as it could, but the fox quickly gobbled it up.

The fox was so busy finishing up that he did not see Shunya sneaking up behind him. The boy jumped on to the fox and tied him to a bigger stone in the pen.

'That's not too bad. Now I have my worm, the duck and the fox.'

~

That same night, a wolf came through the forest. He saw the fox tied up in the pen and smiled to himself. This would be an easy hunt. He pounced on the fox and devoured every last bit of it in less than a minute. But Shunya had seen the wolf before it could get away. He tiptoed to the wolf and knowing he could not fight with it, brought down the axe on it in one clean blow.

The next day, when he told his brothers of his great hunt, they laughed at him loudly, 'What good is a dead wolf? It will stink up the whole house in a few days and we will have to work to bury it deep. You really are a great fool.'

Their insults kept Shunya up the whole night.

'Perhaps my brothers are right. The dead wolf will not last long. I will save the skin instead.'

~

So he skinned the wolf, dried the skin and made a drum from it. No one had a drum as loud as Shunya, and he was very proud of it. Every evening he would go around the town, beating it loudly.

The whole kingdom heard of Shunya's great drum.

One day, the king sent for the boy.

'I would like to borrow your drum for the evening. I am having a feast to announce that suitors may come to seek my daughter's hand in marriage, but there's no instrument as loud as your drum,' the king said.

Shunya was not pleased. He was the only boy from the forest who had not been invited, but Shunya was kind, so he brought the drum to the king's palace nevertheless.

'Be very careful. Do not tear the skin of my drum. I will never get another one like it. My worm, my duck, my fox and my wolf have all helped to make it.'

'I will take good care of it,' the king promised.

~

When Shunya went to get his drum back the next day, the king apologized. He had struck it too hard and it had split open. It was beyond repair. He offered the boy a great price, but Shunya wouldn't have it.

'I do not want your price. I want my drum. Give me back my drum!'

'I can't do that. It has gone forever. I will give you anything you desire in exchange for it.'

'Here is my chance for a good fortune,' thought Shunya. 'Now I will surprise my brothers.'

'Since you cannot give me back my drum, I will take your daughter's hand in marriage instead,' he said to the king.

The king was taken aback by the demand, but true to his word, he gave his daughter in marriage to Shunya.

His brothers were angered, but the mother

said, 'I told you he is wiser than all, and yet you called him Shunya and a fool. You will never gain anything from laughing at someone else.'

The princess brought great treasures with her, and Shunya and she lived happily with the mother, tending to the vegetable garden, gathering wood and carrying water from the stream, while the older brothers were made officers in the king's army for their great shooting skills. It had been a good bargain for everyone after all.

'The brothers worked so hard!' said Abir. 'They deserved to marry the princess!'

'Shunya worked just as hard. In fact, he worked every day while they went to hunt only a few times a year,' said Megha.

'And the two brothers laughed at their little brother and thought highly of themselves,' added Grandpa. 'Only a virtuous boy deserves a princess.'

6

The Youngest Girl to Climb Mount Everest

'I have just the story to inspire us for tomorrow,' said Grandpa, trotting into the kitchen.

Megha, Abir, Grandpa and Dabbu along with Mrs Tomar and Nimbu were preparing for a hike up to Bhadraj Hill the next day. The Internet promised it would be a challenging adventure, and all of them were busy checking off a list of things that their online guide said would be needed.

'Well, tell us then!' said Mrs Tomar, continuing to stuff puris into a hot case.

'No, not like this, aunty,' said Megha. 'We can't be doing other things during Pyjama Story Time.

Abir nodded, 'Yes, we must be in bed.'

'And in pyjamas!'

When they finally sat down, after what seemed like hours, they were exhausted.

'I could do with a story now,' said Megha.

'Yes,' agreed Abir. 'We haven't even begun the hike and I'm already tired.'

'Me too,' murmured Mrs Tomar.

'Wo-woof.'

'Tweet tweet.'

'I think all we need is some hot chocolate and Poorna's tale!' chimed in Grandpa.

It was a cold May evening somewhere in the snow-covered Himalayan range. It had rained in the morning and an angry wind had been blowing all day. Thirteen-year-old Poorna sat

EVEREST BASE CAMP

inside her tent, preparing for her last trek up to Mount Everest.

'Mummy and Papa will be so proud of me when I go back home as the youngest girl ever to climb Mount Everest!' Poorna told herself. 'Tomorrow I must reach the peak.'

She finished her meal of Maggi and milk, and at 9.30 p.m., fully packed and prepped, her twenty-five kilogram bag on her back, she set out on her way to the top of the mountain.

It would be hours of vertical climbing in pitch darkness. Poorna knew it was not going to be easy, but she had to be strong.

'You are my brave girl,' her father had said to her. 'Remember that.'

So UP and UP she went.

Poorna was halfway through the trek when she felt a dizzy spell – the snow in front of her started swimming in circles and she could see stars twinkling in it. She wanted to rest for just a second to avoid falling, but behind her was a sharp drop and in front a steep mountain. There was no place to rest!

'You can do it,' she heard her coach's voice in her head.

She would just have to continue climbing and find a stop ahead.

So UP and UP and UP she went.

When she finally stopped to catch a quick breath, Mount Everest was only a few minutes away.

'I still remember the last fifteen minutes to the peak. I was shaking with excitement. After almost a year of training for it, I would finally be on the highest peak in the world!' Poorna later said.

At 6 a.m. on 25 May 2014, thirteen-year-old Poorna Malavath became the youngest girl to climb Mount Everest.

~

This young girl's training began at the Bhongir Rock Climbing School near her village in Telangana. She was selected for a five-day climbing programme.

'The 29,029-foot Mount Everest never scared me as much as the 750-foot Bhongir Rock!' Poorna laughed.

The rock was Poorna's first-ever climb. Of the 110 climbers that participated, twenty were selected to train to climb the Mount Everest. Poorna stood first among them.

~

The first step was a twenty-day training in Darjeeling. They had to learn to trek in the snow and climb the 17,000-foot Renok Peak.

Training had only begun when Poorna overheard her local coach complaining about the selection of a child, and a girl at that.

But Poorna refused to be discouraged.

'I will show him how good I am at climbing,' she said to herself, and became one of the nine climbers to be selected for the next level – a fifteen-day-long winter expedition to Ladakh.

'This was to train us to climb and live in extreme conditions,' said Poorna.

And extreme it was. All the water they used was frozen, their eyelashes and eyebrows had icicles on them and the winds were piercing cold. Even the local people had migrated to warmer towns nearby.

It was in such weather that they hiked.

'It taught me how many layers to wear so I wouldn't freeze to death!' said Poorna.

Finally, only two people were selected for a special three-month training programme to climb Mount Everest – Poorna and seventeen-year-old Anand Kumar.

~

Three months later, with the final permission to climb Mount Everest in hand, Poorna went back to give her ninth grade exams and seek permission from her parents to go on the next expedition.

'You must go!' her father said.

Her mother, on the other hand, needed a lot of convincing.

'We must gang up on your mother!' her father said to Poorna.

And so after her coach, Shekhar Babu, and mentor, Pravin Kumar, both came to talk to her mother, Poorna was set to start her expedition on 14 April.

~

Poorna's hike to Mount Everest and back took fifty-two days.

'When I looked down from Mount Everest,

all I saw were mountains! It was beautiful and extremely thrilling,' she said.

Of course, the snow all around her was a bonus.

'Snow is heaven!'

~

Poorna has since scaled Mount Kilimanjaro (Africa, 2016), Mount Elbrus (Europe, 2017), Mount Aconcagua (South America, 2019), Mount Cartsnez (Oceania region, 2019) and Mount Vinson Massif (Antarctica, 2019).

She is close to achieving her goal of scaling all the seven tallest summits in the world. Mount Denali (North America's highest mountain peak) is next on her list.

'You were right, Grandpa, I am ready to take on any hill now!' said Abir, jumping up and down.

'Me too!' said Megha.

'Me three!' followed Mrs Tomar.

'Tweet tweet teet.'

'Woof oof.'

The next day, the six of them climbed Bhadraj Hill in record time, and as they sat down to eat their lunch, the world was only made of hills.

7

The Girl Who Wished to Live Forever

As a treat for the great report cards Megha and Abir had received in the mail, Grandpa took the kids for a toy haul.

'You can both have 1000 rupees each. Pick whatever you want from the store, but make sure that it does not exceed your budget,' said Grandpa.

'YES, GRANDPA!' shouted the kids in excitement, eager to begin.

'And remember, I am going to pick up some books for all of us and will be back in half an hour. So you must be done by then.'

'HALF AN HOUR IS PLENTY,' roared Megha.

'YES YES, CAN WE START?'

'Calm down, kids. Okay. On your mark. Get set. GO!'

The kids were off in a dash. Grandpa could hardly keep track of the two as they ran from shelf to shelf, crouching, jumping, choosing and filling their bags with toys.

'Ajay, keep an eye on them, I'll be back,' said Grandpa to the owner of the store.

Ajay nodded.

~

When Grandpa came back, he found Megha and Abir standing by the counter, out of breath and grinning from ear to ear.

'WE MADE IT!'

'I see you did. Have you calculated the total?'

'I have,' said Megha.

Megha's bag of a diary, pens, slime of five sparkly colours, a teddy bear, magic sand and a set of magnets totalled 856 rupees.

Abir's bag of a race car set, Cricket Attax Collection and slime amounted to 1330 rupees!

'That's not fair. I have fewer things than Megha does,' cried Abir.

'You can have my remaining 144 rupees, Abir.'

'But I am still short,' Abir said, looking at Grandpa.

'You will just have to leave behind either the car or the cards.'

After much thinking, Abir exchanged the complete collection of cards for a smaller set.

At Pyjama Story Time, Grandpa found just the story for a sulking Abir – the story of a girl who wanted more.

A long time ago there lived a girl named Sudha. From her family she inherited a lot of wealth and lived a carefree life – no work and only play.

'I would like to live like this for six hundred years,' she thought to herself. 'Healthy and happy. The lifespan of humans is too short.'

She had heard stories of emperors in ancient times who had lived a thousand years, and determined to find their secret, she travelled to all the corners of the world.

Finally, she came across the tale of a king named Bhut-ma.

Bhut-ma was a powerful king whose kingdom spanned far and wide. He built large palaces and larger armies, and accumulated all the riches in the world. He had everything he could wish for, and yet he was miserable.

'Because one day I must die and leave it all,' he said. 'If only I could find the Elixir of Life, I would live a thousand years and be a happy man.'

On hearing this, one of his advisers told him of a hermit named Manna up in the Himalayas. He was said to possess the recipe for the Elixir of Life, a draught that was sure to make the drinker live forever.

King Bhut-ma ordered his adviser to set out for the Himalayas at once and bring him back a bottle of the elixir.

Many months passed before the adviser returned with the elixir for the king, who went on to live for several hundred years. Ever since, the Himalayas have come to be known as the home of the hermits who held the secret of the Elixir of Life and Manna their guardian angel.

~

On hearing of the king's success, Sudha's resolve grew stronger. 'I will scale the Himalayas and find the hermits myself,' she said.

So she left her home and started for the mountains.

For days she travelled across mountains,

walked through rain, hailstorms and snow, but never a hermit did she find.

At last she found a hunter, and asked him, 'Can you tell me where the hermits who have the Elixir of Life live?'

'No,' said the hunter, 'but you can visit the shrine of Manna, the god of the hermits. It is just ahead.'

Delighted, Sudha walked to the shrine, but found no one there. She decided to give up her quest for the hermits and pray to Manna instead.

She prayed for seven days, begging the god to show her the path to the elixir.

On the seventh day, at midnight, the door of the innermost shrine flew open and a shimmering Manna appeared in front of Sudha.

'Your desire is a selfish one and cannot be easily granted. You ask for the hermits' secret elixir, but do you know how hard a hermit's life is? A hermit only eats what has dropped to the ground and lives a life of no wishes. You, Sudha, are fond of a comfortable life of no work. However, you have prayed, and I will help you in some way. I will send you to the Country of Everlasting Life – a country where people live forever!'

Saying this, Lord Manna handed the girl a little paper crane and told her that it would carry her there.

As soon as Sudha sat on the crane, it grew bigger and bigger until it was large enough for her to ride on. Then it spread its wings and flew up high into the sky, over the mountains and the seas.

On and on it flew for thousands of miles until they reached an island, and as soon as Sudha got off, the crane folded up and flew into her pocket.

~

The Country of Everlasting Life! Sudha walked around the country and its towns. Everything was different from her own, but the land and people seemed prosperous, and so she decided to find a house and live on.

No one on the island had ever seen death, and sickness was a thing unknown. Quite unlike Sudha and other ordinary people, instead of fearing death, everyone on the island longed for it. They were tired of their long, long lives.

But deadly poisons had no effect in this country. The poisonous globefish was a popular dish in restaurants and hawkers sold sauces made of dirty cockroaches and flies. Sudha never saw anyone fall ill after eating these horrible things; never did she see anyone with as much as a cold.

One of the medicines that was high in demand at the chemists helped the taker get loosies and a few wrinkles!

The islanders tried to die, but all in vain. A life of no change seemed tiring and sad. The wealthy would have given all their riches to shorten their lives by a few hundred years.

Sudha, on the other hand, was delighted! 'I will never grow tired of living.'

She was the only happy person on the island. She set up a popular business of grey and white hair dyes and could not imagine going back to her native land.

~

Time passed quickly as she worked from morning to night, and before she knew it, three hundred years had flown by.

Soon, Sudha began to grow tired of the country and longed to go back to her own home where she could die.

She sat once again to pray to Lord Manna to take her back.

No sooner had she sat down to pray than the paper crane popped out of her pocket. Sudha was amazed to see that it had remained undamaged after all these years.

Once more Sudha sat on the bird, and it grew and grew until it was large enough for her to ride on. Then it spread its wings and flew, over the seas and the mountains, in the direction of home.

~

They were flying over the sea when a storm broke out, bringing the paper crane crumbling down into the water. Obviously, Sudha fell with it. She splashed around in the angry sea, trying to stay alive. She peered into the distance for some sign of a ship or a shore, but she found neither. Instead, she saw a monstrous shark swim her way.

Just as it came close, ready to chomp her up

in one big bite, Sudha screamed to Manna with all her might.

'OH HELP ME, LORD MANNA! HELP!'

Lo and behold, Sudha was awakened by her own screams. She had fallen asleep during her long prayer in the shrine. Her extraordinary adventures had only been a dream!

Frightened, she was getting up to leave when suddenly the shrine was filled with a bright light. In the light stood a messenger.

'I am sent to you by Lord Manna. In answer to your prayers he helped you see the Country of Everlasting Life. But you got tired there and begged to return so that you could die. The lord tested you and dropped you into the sea to be eaten by a shark, but your desire for death was not real. You asked to be saved. The lord believes it is best for you to return home so you can work hard and live a good life. Give up your silly wants. Now you know that even when all wishes are granted, they do not bring happiness.'

Saying this, the messenger disappeared.

Sudha, too, went back home and, giving up her useless wishes, lived a happy and hard-working life with the lessons she had learnt.

'Thank you for giving me your share, Megha. And thank you for the gifts, Grandpa,' said Abir.

'You think he has learnt *his* lesson?' whispered Grandpa to Megha.

The two laughed and hugged Abir, and they all fell off to sleep.

8

The Giant Cleaning Device

As part of his New Year celebrations, every year Grandpa turned the house upside down for a thorough cleaning. This time Megha and Abir decided to help.

The two asked to be in charge of the storeroom, hoping to find some sort of treasure there.

They had emptied the rickety cupboard, and finding nothing in it to their disappointment, were trying to move it out to inspect the wooden floors for a loose board, like they had read of in books, when it began raining sticks instead.

'AAAHHHH!'

'OW OW OW OW OW!

'MUMMY!'

'AAAAAAAAAAA!'

Grandpa came running to find the two under a bundle of brooms of all shapes and sizes.

He helped them up and out of the room.

'Grandpa, what are all these brooms doing behind the cupboard?' asked Megha, rubbing herself to ease the pain.

'Oh, these were your grandma's brooms.'

'She collected brooms?' Abir probed.

'No, no. These are from when she collected them to clean the attic window. You know the big round one?'

'Yes?'

'Well, it was always dirty because it is hard to reach. So your grandma decided to find another way . . .'

The kids' ears pricked up. They knew this was going to be a great story.

This was many, many years ago. Your grandma and I were getting old, so we decided to quit our jobs and come back home to Landour to reopen the family bookstore that had to be closed when I left.

Luckily we found this house for sale near the shop and bought it. Grandma was in charge of cleaning and setting up the house and I was responsible for fixing up the store.

I opened the bookstore after eight months of hard work, but Grandma was not done yet. She was a stickler for perfection.

It was only a year later, when the whole Pais family came over to celebrate the first anniversary of the reopened bookstore, that Grandma declared the house was ready.

I thought it had looked ready all along, so I believed her, and so did everyone else.

That night, however, she told me the truth. 'It is not over yet!'

'What do you mean? You said it was ready in front of everyone today.'

'That was only because everyone was making fun of how long it is taking and the kids were asking me to take a break and visit them!'

I knew your grandma was very sad, and I had to do something.

'Okay, what is left?' I asked.

'The silly attic window. That's all that's been left for a year now!'

'I don't understand.'

'The house would have been done a year ago if it wasn't for that unreachable attic window! There's just no way to clean it!'

'So you're saying . . .'

'I'VE BEEN TRYING TO CLEAN THE ATTIC WINDOW FOR THE LAST 365 DAYS!' she screamed.

It all made sense! I had often heard her mutter in her sleep, 'How do I do it?' 'Too far, too high.' 'Dirt dirt dirt.' 'It must be reached.' But I always dismissed it as a dream.

~

The next few days went by in a blink. Only once everyone had left did Grandma and I get a chance to talk.

'Why don't you start working at the bookstore with me,' I suggested, hoping it would take her mind off the window. 'On Thursday, when we close the shop, we can both come up with ways to clean the window.'

She did not seem convinced, but agreed.

~

Grandma had tried a few things in the last year, so we had to come with innovative ways.

I suggested using a spray pipe after my recommendation of tying a mop to a drone and rubbing it against the window was turned down.

Surprisingly, she had not tried spraying before. So we went hunting for the longest pipe available.

'This should do the trick,' I thought. Excited to turn this into a success, we came back home and got busy with the fittings.

Once the pipe was connected to the tap in the garden, Grandma stood by it while I took my position right under the attic window.

The plan was this: I would find the right angle under the window and hold the pipe up high above my head with my thumb covering the opening to give it an extra squirt that would reach the window.

'Now,' I screamed.

No water.

'DARLING!' I screamed again. 'Now!'

Some water.

I put down the pipe and walked over to Grandma.

'Is that the full pressure?'

'Yes.'

'Well, that's not going to be enough to reach the window. I'm going to have to call the plumber.'

By the time the plumber fixed the tap, it was nightfall, but we decided to take a shot before going to bed.

I took my position at an angle under the window and screamed to Grandma to turn on the tap.

The pressure had been fixed all right!

'STOP STOP STOP!' I screamed.

The pipe was not aimed correctly and I got drenched.

'Perhaps we should get a ladder for you,' suggested Grandma.

'But there isn't place to rest the really tall one.'

'We'll have to make do with the medium one with four legs.'

The ladder was fetched. I climbed on to it and signalled to Grandma to turn on the tap. Milliseconds later, I called out to her to turn it off, again.

The ladder had done nothing, and I was even more drenched than the first time. I went to bed shivering and woke up with a cold.

~

On our way to the bookstore the next day, I gathered all the courage to make my next suggestion to Grandma.

'Darling . . . how . . . how about we call a professional window cleaner?' I said. I was beginning to wonder if we could come up with anything that would not only reach the window but also successfully clean it.

'No.'

'Why not. It will be done within an hour or less.'

'No.'

'But . . .'

'It is our home and we must clean it properly ourselves,' she said sternly, and I left it at that.

~

I thought long and hard before I made my next suggestion, but Grandma had come up with a plan of her own by then.

'We need to fashion a giant cleaning device,' she said.

'A what?'

'Don't worry. I know what I'm doing,' she said. She sure seemed to have a great plan, so I didn't probe further.

'I'll come back at lunchtime to help you,' I said.

~

On my way back at lunchtime, I bumped into Grandma running out of the neighbour's house with brooms in both hands.

'Do they know you're running away with their brooms?' I laughed.

'Don't tease me, come and help!' Grandma smiled.

We walked into the garden that was already stacked with at least twenty brooms of all shapes and sizes.

'What is the plan?' I asked.

'We're going to make a giant cleaning device! Help me tie all these brooms in a straight line, will you?'

'Why are we not using sticks instead with a broom at the end?'

'Because I thought of using brooms!' said Grandma, getting angry.

I didn't ask any more questions and we got to work, tying them all up. I want you to imagine this giant cleaning device – twenty or so brooms tied one after the other, with a cloth tied at one end. It truly was one of a kind.

And it was time to test it out.

Grandma and I held it up.

'ONE, TWO, THREE, HOIST!'

The giant cleaning device rose up in the air and reached close to the window.

'IT'S WORKING! IT'S WORKING!'

But the veranda roof that protruded under the attic caused an obstruction.

'We need the ladder.'

Once again the medium-sized ladder was fetched and I climbed on to it. Once again the giant cleaning device was hoisted. We cannot tell if the device would have reached, because no sooner had we lifted it up than it plopped and hung in a sad C.

We brought it down and tried tying it together more tightly, but every time it was held up for more than a few seconds, it hunched its back and plopped back into a C.

'OH, JUST GET RID OF THE VERANDA ROOF!' Grandma yelled.

'Darling, imagine the dust that would come into the veranda and spread all over the house then!' I said, trying to lighten her mood.

It did not help. She dropped the broom and went in, huffing.

'I think we should make this into an L-shaped device and try cleaning from the upstairs window,' I said, following her in. 'The distance will be shorter and we'll also be able to hold it up for longer.'

Grandma didn't say a word so I continued, 'Yes, I think that might work. We can try that tonight.'

~

Now, the most important thing to know about our house is that it is perched at the edge of a hill and you have to walk around the corner to reach the neighbours. This brings me to the second important thing – the sounds in our house do not travel to them.

So no one heard Grandma scream until I got back from work that night.

'PAT PAT!' Grandma's scream echoed as I walked in.

'PEA! Where are you?'

I looked around the garden but couldn't see her anywhere. I went into the house and she sure wasn't inside because her voice was faint there.

'PAT!'

I ran outside with a torch.

'UP HERE, YOU GOOSE!'

I pointed the torch up at the house and there she was – stuck on the roof of the veranda, the giant cleaning device in her hand.

'HOW DID YOU GET THERE?'

'I DECIDED TO TRY USING THE

DEVICE FROM THE UPSTAIRS WINDOW LIKE YOU HAD SUGGESTED.'

'WELL, I ALSO SAID L-SHAPE AND THAT I WOULD COME AND HELP!'

'CAN'T YOU SEE IT IS AN L? IT'S THE LEG OF THE L THAT GOT CAUGHT ON THE ROOF AND SAVED ME!'

'WELL, GENIUS IDEA, THEN!'

'PAT, CAN YOU GET ME DOWN BEFORE YOU MOCK ME?'

'OKAY. BUT ON ONE CONDITION.'

'Hmm,' Grandma said, and I took that as a yes.

'YOU ARE NOT GOING TO DO THIS ALONE AGAIN.'

'OKAY OKAY.'

~

I finally got her down and made her some of her favourite soup. She had managed to construct the

L-shape soon after I left, which meant that she had been stuck on the roof for hours! She refused to tell me exactly how long she was up there.

That night I decided it was time to take matters into my own hands. So when Grandma fell asleep, and it was a deep sleep after the long day she had had, I sneaked out and went over to a local painter's house.

He was befuddled by the task at first, but agreed to come. It took him less time to clean the window than it did for us to tie the brooms together.

When Grandma woke up in the morning, she was shocked to see the window sparkling clean.

'How did you do it?' she asked.

I did not reveal my secret, and she was just relieved not to have to think of it. Ever since, I have called the painter twice a month at midnight to come clean the attic window.

Megha and Abir were rolling on the floor laughing by the time Grandpa came to the end of the story.

'Grandpa, you said you *have* called the painter ever since,' said Megha after a while.

'Yes.'

'Does that mean you still call him at midnight twice a month?'

'Good girl, you know your grammar well.' Grandpa smiled.

9

The Hare and the Lion

'You'll be squished in a day then, won't you?' said Megha.

'That doesn't even happen to him in the movie!' screamed Abir.

'Well, it will happen to you in real life. Here's a live example, Mr Timon,' Megha yelled and jumped on Abir.

Grandpa walked in on the two scratching and beating each other up and had to pry them away. 'What do you think you two are doing?'

'Having a real-life Lion King fight!' squeaked Abir.

'You should thank Grandpa for saving your

life. You can barely get a word out,' scoffed Megha.

The two of them had watched *The Lion King* over lunch.

'And why is there no peace in my forest?' interrupted Grandpa.

'Well, we were talking about which Lion King character we want to be. I chose Simba, and Abir decided he wanted to be Timon.'

'But why is that a reason for unrest?'

'I'm going to be the king of the jungle, Grandpa. I was just showing Abir what happens to tiny animals like him.'

'That's not always true,' said Grandpa.

'Yes, tell her, Grandpa. That's what I was saying,' said Abir.

'I will tell you both why I say so, but before I do, you shall both go and wash up, you stinky animals.'

It was early in the morning. A hare, let's call him Timon, was roaming the forest in search of food when he stumbled upon a willow tree buzzing with bees. He looked up to find the biggest honeybee nest he had ever seen.

'It's autumn, the honey must be ready and juicy,' said Timon to himself. 'I'm not one for honey, but that nest will surely have a gooey, yummy honeycomb, and who can resist that!'

He decided he would need help in getting to the honeycomb and went in search of a friend.

He was crossing Moosa's hole when the big rat invited him in.

'Moosa might be a good choice,' Timon thought.

So after a few minutes of chit-chat, he said, 'Moosa, I have found the juiciest honeybee nest, but I need your help chasing the bees out of it. I am happy to share the honey if you will come help.'

Who could resist a pulpy honeycomb?

When the two reached the willow tree, Timon pointed to the nest and said, 'We will have to smoke the bees out before we can eat the honey.'

Moosa nodded. The two collected some straw, climbed up to the nest, lit the straw and smoked the bees out and away.

They were in the middle of their feast when who should come but the lion who lived under that tree; let's call him Simba.

'Who is it that is up there,' he roared. You see, Simba's eyesight was weak and he had forgotten to wear his glasses.

Timon, on the other hand, could see Simba clearly, and whispered to Moosa, 'Don't say anything, that old fellow is crazy. He'll eat us up in no time.'

'Who are you? Speak now!' Simba roared louder.

This scared Moosa and he squeaked, 'It's just us!'

'Now you've done it,' said Timon, but an expert in escape, he came up with a plan the very next second. 'Wrap me up in straw, tell Simba to keep out of the way and throw me down.'

'What about me?'

'When you come down, Simba will ask you who was with you. You tell him I had brought you here because honey would help with your painful, smelly tummy. He will surely keep away from you because of it.'

Moosa did exactly as he was told. He wrapped Timon up in straw and called to Simba, 'Stand back. I am going to throw this straw down and then come down myself.'

When Moosa came down as promised, Simba asked him exactly what Timon had said, 'Who was up there with you?'

'Why, it was Timon the hare. Didn't you see him when I threw him down?'

'I didn't,' Simba screamed and began searching for the hare. Of course, Timon had long found the right moment to run away.

'He must be around. He brought me here because honey helps me with my bad, smelly tummy,' continued Moosa.

On hearing this, Simba once again did exactly as Timon had predicted.

'Get away from me, you filthy animal,' he scoffed and dashed away.

~

Timon waited for three days before inviting Tinda the turtle for the second round of the honey feast. After all, they could not finish all the honey the first time.

'Is the honey yours?' asked Tinda suspiciously.

'Of course,' said Timon.

'It is too, I smoked out the bees,' he thought to himself.

'All right, then,' Tinda said eagerly, and off the two went.

They were in the middle of the feast when Simba, who had been keeping an eye out for Timon since the last time, stepped out.

'Who is it that is stealing my honey?' he inquired. He had forgotten to wear his glasses again!

Timon asked Tinda to keep quiet. 'Don't say anything or he'll eat us up in no time.'

But when Simba repeated his question, Tinda became wary.

'You said this was your honey, is it Simba's?'

'Well, technically, it's the forest's honey. Anyone can eat it. The lion just wants to believe it is his because he lives under the tree,' said Timon.

The turtle was angry at being tricked, and

when Simba called out again, he answered, 'It's only us.'

'Come down, then,' Simba said.

'We're coming,' he replied again.

'I've got Timon this time,' thought Simba.

Seeing that they were in trouble again, Timon said, 'Tinda, wrap me up in the straw, tell Simba to stand out of the way and then throw me down. I'll wait for you below. He can't hurt you in your shell.'

'This hare wants to run away and leave me to the lion. I'll make sure he gets caught first and the lion is full with him,' Tinda thought to himself. And so he agreed to Timon's plan.

Once he had bundled Timon up, he called out, 'Timon is coming!' and threw him down.

Simba immediately caught the hare and said, 'Now what shall I do with you?'

'You can't eat me,' said Timon.

'And why is that?'

'It's no use. My skin is awfully tough. It is all the hard gourd my mother made me eat. You can try whirling me around and knocking me against the ground to soften me.'

This sounded like a good plan to Simba. He took the hare by his tail and whirled him around. But just as he was going to knock him on the ground, Timon slipped out of his grasp and ran away.

Angry and disappointed, Simba turned to Tinda, 'You come down now.'

Tinda did as he was told. When Simba saw the turtle, he said, 'Now you're a hard one to eat. Tell me how to make you edible.'

Learning from Timon, Tinda said, 'Oh, that's easy. You just have to lay me in the mud on the riverbank and rub my back with your paw until my shell comes off.'

On hearing this, Simba carried Tinda to the bank, placed him in the mud and began to rub his back. But soon the tortoise replaced himself with a piece of rock and slipped away. The lion continued to scrub until his paws were raw. When he glanced down at them, he realized that he had been tricked yet again!

Furious, he yelled, 'THE HARE HAS FOOLED ME AGAIN, BUT I'LL GO HUNT HIM DOWN.'

So Simba set out immediately in search of Timon.

He went through the forest asking everyone if they knew where Timon lived, but the hare had recently moved house and no one knew the new address.

Simba, however, went along, continuing his inquiries until a sparrow answered, 'That's his house on the top of the mountain.'

Without any delay, the lion climbed the mountain and reached the house that he was told was Timon's. But there was no one there.

'Even better,' Simba said to himself. 'I will hide inside and when Timon returns I will pounce on him and eat him up.'

In a matter of a few hours along came a skipping Timon, unaware of the danger. He was about to enter the house when he discovered paw marks leading inside.

'Ah! Mr Lion is inside, is he?' he thought to himself. Then, tiptoeing back a little, he called out, 'Fine day, house? How are you?'

Waiting a moment, he said, 'Well, this is strange. You always ask me how I am in return. There must be someone inside today.'

When Simba heard this he called out, 'How are you, dear Timon?'

Timon burst out laughing and shouted, 'Oh, Mr Simba! *You're* inside, and I bet you want to eat me. But first, tell me, where have you heard of a talking house!'

Enraged at being fooled yet again, Simba replied, 'YOU JUST WAIT TILL I GET HOLD OF YOU! YOU JUST WAIT!'

'Oh, I think *you'll* have to do the waiting,' cried Timon and ran away, Simba chasing after him.

But the lion never caught up with the sprightly hare. Exhausted, he said, 'I don't want to have anything more to do with him,' and returned to his home under the willow tree.

'Ha! See, you couldn't even catch me,' shot Abir.

'Well, honestly, I'm sure Megha can catch you easily, Abir.' Grandpa laughed. 'This was just to say that I, too, believe Timon is cooler than Simba!'

10

The Man Who Invented the Chocolate Bar

Megha and Abir had spent all evening in the kitchen, making Grandpa a special chocolate something for his birthday the next day. Even dinner was delivered by Mrs Tomar – a special mango chicken curry and rice – since the kids were way too busy and Grandpa was not allowed anywhere near the kitchen.

'This is the perfect dinner to have before our dessert!' said Megha, heating up the curry in the microwave.

'Yes! Do you think the dessert is ready?' chirped Abir, peeking into the fridge.

'It should be by the time we've finished dinner. Now stop opening the fridge again and again and call Grandpa to the table. I'll get the food.'

~

At the table, Grandpa had barely put his spoon down after a hearty meal than the kids jumped up.

'WE'LL BE RIGHT BACK, GRANDPA!'

'RIGHT BACK!'

Grandpa nodded with a smile. This was the second kitchen treat he would receive from the kids for his birthday. Last year it had been a pizza as big as the table! He wondered what it would be today.

'GRANDPA, CLOSE YOUR EYES PLEASE AND PUT YOUR HANDS OUT!' Abir called out.

'So it's something *normal-sized*,' Grandpa thought with relief.

'OKAY, YOU CAN OPEN YOUR EYES NOW!'

In Grandpa's hands was a bar of chocolate as big as a TV! The kids had frozen each brick and pieced it together right before packing it for him. 'Pais's Mango Cream-Filled Chocolate: Premium Handcrafted Chocolate With a Creamy Mango Surprise in the Centre' read the yellow paper strip over the foil with a drawing of a mango oozing chocolate.

'My two favourite things!' Grandpa beamed.

'OH, OPEN IT ALREADY, GRANDPA!' screamed the kids.

It was Grandpa's favourite Cadbury Silk chocolate melted and filled with the creamiest mango syrup and set again, with a stamped logo for Pais!

'WELL, LET'S DIVE IN!' Grandpa, too, exclaimed in excitement.

The three of them took a corner each and got up only once it was over and their clothes were coloured yellow and brown.

'Now that was the best birthday gift ever,' Grandpa said, hugging the two kids. 'You guys are my two Joseph Frys.'

'Who's Joseph Fry, Grandpa?'

And there it was, the story for the day.

A long, long time ago, in Wiltshire, United Kingdom, there lived a boy named Joseph Fry. By the time he was twenty-five years old, Joseph was a renowned doctor and an apothecary in the neighbouring town of Bristol.

The year was 1753. Bristol was a large port where ships filled with all kinds of things arrived and left all day long.

One of the things that came in was cocoa!

Now, the cacao bean, from which cocoa powder is made, from which chocolate is produced, was first grown in America over 5000 years ago. Some say it is even older than that! But this is not a history lecture; this is the story of Joseph Fry and how he went on to make the world's first chocolate bar.

Joseph first began buying and selling the bitter cocoa flakes for its health benefits.

It can (remember these so you can tell your parents):

1. Prevent cancer
2. Improve blood pressure
3. Improve heart health
4. Keep the skin healthy
5. Help in digestion
6. Even possibly improve teeth health!

He believed in it so much that he set up a factory to grind the cocoa flakes to a fine powder and produce a velvety drink! Hot chocolate, you say!?

~

When he died years later, his son, named Joseph Storrs Fry (or Joseph Fry II), took over the business.

'I will make J.S. Fry and Sons the biggest name in cocoa,' he said.

He followed in the footsteps of his father, and by 1824 the Frys were selling almost half of the country's cocoa!

But the greatest contribution of the family to the history of chocolate was yet to come.

~

The family began to experiment with chocolate when the three sons of Joseph Fry II – Richard, Frances and Joseph (again) – took over the business.

The first was the addition of a powder to absorb some of the oil in cocoa and make it less bitter.

'Let's call it Pearl Cocoa!' they said. 'The powder looks like tiny brown pearls.'

Pearl Cocoa was cheaper and was bought by everyone. Fry became a famous name.

Then came THE day, when the three brothers, sitting at the table, working on a new invention, made chocolate!

It was 1847, almost hundred years since Joseph Fry first began selling cocoa powder. The brothers were experimenting in the factory when one of them, we don't know which one, said, 'I wonder if we should try mixing cocoa powder with cocoa fat and some sugar to make it solid.'

'WHY NOT!' said another one. Again, we don't know which one, but the brothers were very supportive of this idea.

And so they did. The paste they mixed was left in a container to set. THAT was the world's first solid chocolate!

FRY'S CHOCOLATE

'This is brilliant!'

'People can carry it in their pocket everywhere!'

'Mmmmm . . . YUMMY TOO!'

Next they moulded it into a bar – the world's first chocolate bar! Before this chocolate had always been drunk, never eaten. CAN YOU EVEN IMAGINE A WORLD WITHOUT CHOCOLATE BARS?

By 1866, the Frys had made their first creamy chocolate.

Two years later, a company we know well, Cadbury Brothers, began making a similar bar.

In 1875, Daniel Peter from Switzerland along with Henry Nestlé, another familiar name, invented the milk chocolate. Daniel used Nestlé's invention of thickened milk to mix with cocoa powder and sugar. This resulted in a soft, sweet chocolate bar.

The chocolate bar was brought back to America by Milton Hershey in 1900.

As we all know, there have been many new inventions in chocolate ever since. The US alone produces 40,000 different kinds of chocolate candy bars!

The Frys could not keep up with so much competition. The company was soon sold off to Cadbury, but the Fry family continued to be known as the inventors of the chocolate bar.

'Imagine if we couldn't eat chocolate!' said Megha.

'I'd just drink it in everything then – milk, water, dal,' quipped Abir.

'I wonder if our bar is a new invention?' he continued.

'Well, you'll just have to find out or keep making new ones until you stumble upon a brand-new invention!' concluded Grandpa.

11

The Two Sisters

'I want to hear a story about a girl,' said Megha.

'EWWWWWWWWWWWWWWWWW, I refuse to listen to a girly story!' Abir protested.

'We've only had a couple of stories about girls – neither of them *girly* – and so many about boys.'

'We've had stories about animals, too,' Abir remarked.

'But I want a story about a girl.'

'Oh, I think I can see a story about two girls that might please you both,' said Grandpa as he peered into the suitcase.

'Whatever.' Abir was not convinced.

'Yay!' Megha danced with joy. 'That's perfect.'

Deep in the forests of Meghalaya, there once lived two twin sisters who were as different as day and night. One of the sisters was good and the other was positively horrid.

They were only thirteen when their parents fell mighty sick and ALL the responsibility fell on the sisters.

Debbie, being the good sister, said cheerfully, 'I will go and find a job first, sister. You stay home and take care of our parents.'

So she packed her bag, kissed everyone goodbye and went off in the direction of the forest. She was skipping through the woods when she came upon a bakery with an oven full of loaves.

'Little girl! Little girl!' the loaves cried. 'Take us out! Take us out or we shall soon be burnt, we've been in the oven for years!'

Debbie, being a kind girl, put down her bag and took out the bread. 'You will be golden and fluffy now,' she said, before going on her way.

She had not gone too far when she heard someone call out to her again.

'Little girl! Milk me, please. I have been waiting for a long time and no one has come to my help. Milk me immediately!'

It was a crying cow. So Debbie put down her bag again and milked the cow. 'Now you shall be more comfortable,' she said, and went on her way.

Then she came to an apple tree covered in the juiciest of apples. So crowded was the tree that its branches were drooping with the weight.

'Little girl! Little girl! Please shake my branches. The apples are so heavy, I cannot stand straight.'

'Of course,' said gentle Debbie and got to work. She shook the branches until all the apples fell to the ground and the tree stood straight.

'You'll have no back pain now,' she said.

~

Debbie journeyed on uninterrupted until she came to the house of a very old witch. The witch had been looking for a maid and promised Debbie good pay. So the little girl agreed to stay.

All day long Debbie worked around the house. She dusted, swept and cooked in the morning; in the evenings she tended to the vegetable garden and combed all the witch's brooms and her curly long hair. She even had to make sure that the fire under the cauldron was always bright and cheery!

There was only one thing she did not do – clean the chimney, because she was strictly told not to.

'You must never go near the chimney,' said the witch. 'Never must you sweep it, and never must you look up. If you do, something evil will fall on you and you will meet a bad end.'

~

For years Debbie worked and never a rupee did she see. The little girl wanted to go home to visit her parents and sister, but how could she go without her wages? So she continued to work diligently.

One day she was dreaming about her family and sweeping the floor when she saw soot falling down the chimney. Debbie bent down immediately to clean it, and down plopped something into her lap. Only, it was a big bag full of money!

The witch was out hunting for lizards for her evening brew and Debbie thought it was a fine opportunity to run off home.

She quickly packed her bag and sneaked out of the back door, but she had only gone a little way when she heard the swishing of the witch's broomstick.

Debbie saw the apple tree she had helped nearby and ran to it.

'Oh apple tree, the old witch is after me!

She'll pick my bones,

And bury me in stones.

Hide me please till I am free?'

'Of course, kind girl. You helped me when I was in need and one good deed deserves another.'

So the apple tree picked her up and hid her in its leafy branches.

When the witch flew by and asked if the apple tree had seen her little maid, the tree answered, 'No, dear witch, not for seven years!'

'Oh, that little beastly doll.

She's stolen my money, bag and all!' she cried and flew the wrong way.

Soon after, little Debbie got down, thanked the tree for being so kind and went on her way home.

She was greeting the cow she had met earlier when she heard the witch's laugh close by.

'Hehehehehehehehehhehehehhehehhehehe hehehhehehehehehehehehеh!'

'Oh cow, the old witch is after me!

She'll pick my bones,

And bury me in stones.

Hide me please till I am free.'

'Certainly,' answered the cow. 'You milked me and made me comfortable. Hide behind me and I'll keep you safe.'

When the witch flew by and inquired if the cow had seen a little girl, the cow answered, 'No, dear witch, not for seven years!'

'Oh, that little beastly doll.

She's stolen my money, bag and all!' she cried and flew the wrong way.

Little Debbie quickly sneaked out from behind the cow, milked her again as a thank you and continued on her way home.

She was rounding the corner to where she had helped the loaves out of the oven when she heard the swish of the witch's broom again.

'Oh oven, the old witch is after me!
She'll pick my bones,
And bury me in stones.
Hide me please till I am free.'

The oven shook his head, 'I'm afraid there is no room in me; I'm filled to the brim with loaves. Why don't you ask the baker?'

Now the baker was out delivering his loaves, but he was a dear friend of mine and I was visiting him when little Debbie came along.

'I will help you. The baker told me how you saved his last batch of loaves from being burnt, so run into the bakehouse and you will be quite safe there. I will take care of the witch for you,' I said.

When the witch flew by and asked if I had seen her little maid, I answered, 'Look in the oven, she may be there.'

The witch quickly got off her broom and peered into the oven, but she could not see anyone.

'Why don't you go in and look in the farthest corner,' I said cunningly, and as the witch crept over the loaves and in – BANG!

I shut the door in her face.

There she sat, roasting. When she came out with the bread, she was all crisp and brown. She had to scrape her crusty skin off!

And so kind little Debbie got home safe with her bag of money.

~

Debbie's parents jumped with joy on seeing their daughter return, the bag full of money only adding to their delight, but Debbie's twin,

Angelin, was very jealous of her sister's fortune and vowed to get a bag of money for herself.

So she packed her bags and set out for the witch's house.

On her way she crossed the oven where the loaves begged her to take them out because they had been baking for years and were bound to burn.

'A likely story.' Angelin laughed. 'So I should burn my fingers to save your crust? No thank you!'

She had only gone a few more metres when the cow called out to her, 'Little girl! Milk me please. I have been waiting and waiting and no one has come to help. Milk me!'

The cruel little girl laughed. 'You can wait some more for all I care. I'm not your milkmaid.'

Saying this she went ahead until she came to the apple tree overburdened by fruit.

'Little girl! Little girl! Please shake my

branches. The apples are so heavy, I cannot stand straight,' it said.

But Angelin just giggled and plucking one ripe apple, said, 'One is enough for me.'

With that she went on, her tummy filled, and stopped only at the witch's house.

~

Now the witch, as you can imagine, was dreadfully angry with all little girls and made sure that little Angelin did not trick her. For a very long time she stayed in the house, never letting the little girl out of her sight. Poor Angelin had to do all the work and never got a chance to look up the chimney as she had planned.

Until, one day, when the witch ran out of raccoons around the house and had to go searching for them in the forest.

Angelin seized the chance to look up the chimney and, sure enough, a big bag of money fell into her lap!

Well, what was next? Angelin didn't wait another second. She dashed out of the house and into the forest on her way back home.

She was near the apple tree when she heard the witch call, 'I AM GOING TO GET YOU, YOU LITTLE BEAST!'

So she cried as her sister had,

'Oh apple tree, the old witch is after me!
She'll pick my bones,
And bury me in stones.
Hide me please till I am free.'

But the tree said, 'No room here, I have too many apples.'

With no place to hide, Angelin had no choice but to continue running.

Soon the witch came flying by on her broomstick and asked if the apple tree had seen her little maid.

'Yes, dear witch. She's gone that way,' the tree pointed.

Obviously, the witch caught up with little Angelin, gave her a good beating, took the bag of money and sent her home with nothing to show for all the dusting and sweeping and combing and scrubbing and cooking she had done for years.

'Did you hear the loaves talk, Grandpa?' Abir asked.

'No, the baker said they were asleep when I was visiting.'

'Well, they couldn't have been in the oven for years.'

'You're right about that. But I do know that little Debbie got them out at just the right time so they never got burnt!'

'And did you really shut the witch in the oven?'

'Well, I had to, didn't I? She needed to be taught a lesson.'

'And what about the cows and trees, do they really talk?'

'So many questions today! Of course, they do! You just have to listen to them patiently. They may not speak your language, but I'm certain you'll understand them. You understand Dabbu and he understands you, no?'

'That's true!' said Abir, and let Dabbu plant a wet kiss on his face.

12

The Boy Who Loved Cheese

Grandpa's was an old house and he, an old man. And while he made sure everything was in order and absolutely clean, because he was certain Grandma would haunt him otherwise, he did have a soft corner for the little mice he let hide in holes around the house. Even Dabbu was friends with them!

Grandpa was so fond of them that every few days he went to the market to buy cheese for them.

One morning, Megha and Abir went with Grandpa and bought extra cheese for themselves and the mice babies that had just been born.

So, obviously, cheese was on their minds

at Pyjama Story Time when they chanted CHEESE CHEESE CHEESE CHEESE as Grandpa stuck his head into the suitcase.

You know by now that Grandpa found what he was looking for really quickly. And out he came with a stinky old piece of cheese.

He laughed. 'This one is going to be about a boy who loved cheese so much he'd even eat this!'

Twelve-year-old Babbi lived in the greenest hills of the country. He was shorter and stouter than all other boys his age and had rosy, plump cheeks, which his mother said were a result of all the cheese he ate.

And he ate a lot of it! You see, Babbi was a cow herder's son, which meant milk and everything made from it was available in plenty, but his favourite was the creamy, nutty cheese his mother made. Poor woman, she had to make a batch every day!

Babbi liked cheese with every meal. He began with chapattis and butter for breakfast with a side of milk and cheese. Lunch was usually rice, dal, vegetables and some sweet with a side of cheese. And dinner was chapattis and vegetables with a glass of milk and, obviously, a side of cheese. For every meal Babbi's mother gave him three slices, and at every meal the boy complained that the slices were too thin and asked for an extra one.

Every morning, with the help of her husband, Babbi's mother made butter and milk sweets and trays of Babbi's favourite cheese.

But the cheese was never enough.

In every other way Babbi was a good boy. He was obedient at home and in school, helpful to everyone and hard-working. It was only at the table that he was a glutton.

'I think your stomach has a well in it!' his father often said.

~

Babbi had three sisters whom he loved dearly, mostly because they were almost always willing to give him one of their slices of cheese.

One evening, after a well-deserved scolding, Babbi dragged himself up the hill, moping and crying. His sisters, hungry after helping their mother around the house, had refused to share their slices of cheese, and he had poked them until they gave in. All their slices along with all of his had made his stomach hurt horribly, and tired of her greedy son, the mother had given the boy an earful.

Babbi was halfway up when a violent wind shook everything. He quickly sat down under a tree and hid his face in his hands, waiting for it to pass. He could almost hear the wind whisper in his ear as it blew around him.

'There's plenty of cheese here. Come with us . . .'

Afraid, he opened one eye to sneak a peek.

Right in front was a bright light. It looked like a thousand fireflies huddled up in one big ball that was growing by the second. Soon Babbi heard the whisper grow louder and . . .

'Those look too big to be fireflies,' Babbi said to himself.

He got up and walked closer to the ball of light. Could it be the ladies of the woods his mother had told him of? Or one of the fairy rings he had seen far in the hills? So focused was the boy as he walked closer to the light that he forgot all about the scolding he had received.

'Come, we have more than enough cheese for you.' Babbi heard the whisper again.

The ball of light grew BIGGER and BIGGER until at its BIGGEST it was the most gigantic fairy ring Babbi had ever seen.

Indeed! Little fairies were fluttering all around, and they were all dancing to a song.

'Come, little Babbi, come along,

To the world where there are more cheese slices than you can count!'

Soon Babbi felt himself being pulled by the strongest of the fairies.

'You must dance with us,' they said.

'Come, little Babbi, come along,

Here's a world where there are more cheese slices than you can count.

You can eat all day, why, you can eat all night long,

We'll even make you a bed of cheese to mount!'

So catchy was the song that Babbi began to dance with the fairies. He danced and skipped till the first ray of sunlight hit the hill. Then he dropped down, tired, ready to eat the cheese that he had been promised.

The fairies, being honest, got to work, bringing Babbi pile after pile of cheese.

With no mother to scold him and no father to tell him how much cheese to eat, Babbi gobbled slice after cube after slice. There were cheeses of all kinds – stringy and nutty and hard and soft and flaky and creamy and crumbly and fruity and yellow and white and brown and blue and airy and young and old. The fairies kept filling his plate until they could fill no more and so they began piling the cheese around little Babbi until there were walls of cheese around him as high as his house.

By and by Babbi wanted to stop eating and rest a while. His jaws were tired and his stomach felt heavier than an elephant.

At last, with a thick slice of cheese in one hand and a big chunk in the other, he said he could not eat any more. He wanted to go for a walk. He put down the cheese to pull himself up when he heard a wall far away come tumbling down. He looked for a way out, but there were walls all around. One by one the walls started falling until the one right in front of Babbi came down on the poor boy.

'AAAAAAAAAAAAAAAAAAAA AAAAAHHHHHHHHHHHHHH HHHHHHH,' Babbi screamed and fell down, and was crushed under the cheese.

~

Babbi woke up with a start under the tree. His clothes were wet with dew and in his mouth was some grass he had been chewing on greedily.

He got up and rushed back home, promising never to tell anyone about the dream. But, from that day on, Babbi never asked for an extra slice of cheese and was always happy with what he got.

Grandpa finished the story and looked at the kids who were already sound asleep.

'A great lesson wasted.' He laughed and kissed Megha, Abir and Dabbu goodnight before going to bed himself.

13

Two-Year-Old Truptraj and His Tabla

The mood in the Pais House was very dull. There was an unusual silence as Megha and Abir went about the house, packing to go back to school and their parents in Dehradun after two months of winter vacation. Meanwhile, Grandpa was scuttling around town trying to prepare a massive surprise Pyjama Story Time feast for everyone.

Mrs Tomar was invited, as was her parrot, Nimbu. He had even invited Abir's best friend, Kartik, and Megha's best friend, Arjun. They were eight in total, pets and all.

With Mrs Tomar's help, Grandpa had stitched together the blankets, made a tent as big as a room and decorated it with fairy lights. They had placed mattresses in a circle and in the centre was a feast like no one had ever seen! There were pizzas from Tavern, a gooey chocolate fudge cake from Mia's, heaps of cheese balls and chips and marshmallows and caramel toffees, mugs full of hot chocolate with whipped cream, crispy fries, blueberry pancakes, chicken fingers, coleslaw sandwiches, mac and cheese, the kids' favourite momo and so much more. It was a party and would be made up of everything that the kids liked, Grandpa had decided, and he was sure they didn't want pumpkin soup, even though his was lip-smackingly good.

The stage set, all four kids were blindfolded and brought in. You can imagine their excitement when they opened their eyes. It really was a feast!

Of course, everyone began eating immediately, and only stopped when they could eat no more. Even Nimbu, who was picking the cheese off the pizza and the blueberries off the pancakes, and Dabbu, who had gobbled up almost all the momo and chicken fingers, were lying on their backs, holding their tummies.

'Okay!' said Grandpa, pulling up his suitcase. 'Now for story time in the Pyjama Story Time feast!

'YES! WOOF WOOF! CHIRP! Fine then,' said everyone in unison, and so Grandpa began.

GLUG!

DHADHANG DHOOP!

kesariyo rang tane lagyo re lol . . .

DHAM DHAM DHAM!

DHAP!

jini jini jari o melavo re lya garaba . . .

TANG THUP!

jini jini jari o melavo re lol . . .

TADHADHANG!

On the kitchen floor, one-and-a-half-year-old Truptraj Pandey was concentrating on the pots and pans, trying to match the beat with his grandma, who was singing Gujarati songs while rolling out rotis for lunch.

'*Kesariyoooooooooooooooooooo*,' she sang, the roti puffing up as if filled with her Os.

The musical performance was an everyday affair. Truptraj's grandma enjoyed singing while working and Truptraj enjoyed playing on his carefully selected pots and pans. Every time she went into the kitchen or around the house cleaning, Truptraj followed close behind, dragging his instruments.

This was the beginning of the little boy's love for the tabla.

'Our boy has been born with rhythm!' his parents soon realized and enrolled him for tabla classes.

Truptraj practised day and night (he wasn't going to school yet) and began accompanying his grandma on his new dholki instead.

~

The little boy picked up the beats of the tabla in a matter of months, and at only two was invited to give his first performance!

'Papa had to prop me up on two fat cushions just to get me up to the height of the table.' Truptraj laughed.

A year later, he performed on All India Radio. Only three years old, he became the youngest tabla artist to enter the *Guinness World Records*!

~

Of course, Truptraj started school soon and no longer had all the time to practise, but he made sure to set aside at least one hour every day.

'I want to be a world-famous musician one day,' he said, 'and I will with my best friend, the tabla!'

~

Truptraj continues to perform across the country, and his guru has taught him everything there is to know of the tabla.

He even received the Bal Shakti Puraskar from the President of India, Ram Nath Kovind, at only twelve years of age!

'My beat now sounds like **dhin** dhin / *dhage tiraki Ta* / **tu** na / *kat* tin/ **dhage** *tiraki Ta* / **dhi** na,' says Truptraj.

He has given more than 200 performances and is on his way to becoming the next . . .

'Ustad Zakir Hussain!' He jumps. 'The man is unbeatable!'

The only difference is that he wants to mix classical beats with modern music, like his new piece that is a mix of a classical taal and Ed Sheeran's 'Shape of You'!

'Wow!' said Mrs Tomar, who had been drumming her bloated stomach throughout.

'I'm thinking, I could become a chef now!'

'Same! Well, a journalist.'

'I'll be a scientist!' said Kartik.

'And I a businessman!' said Arjun.

Grandpa looked at all of them, smiling and satisfied, thinking, 'Job well done.'

Epilogue

The next day, after a breakfast of cold pizzas and cereal pancakes, the kids bid a tearful goodbye to their grandpa.

'We don't want to go!' Abir cried.

'Of course you do!' said Grandpa. 'Don't you want to meet all your friends at school and have Monodeal parties? And Megha, I'm sure you want to get back to the Famous Four and investigate the next tree killing in the neighbourhood.'

'Well, yes, but we don't want to leave YOU.'

'Yes!'

'Why don't you come with us?'

'I'll come visit in a month or so. And how about I stay until your Easter holidays?'

'YES YES YES!'

'All right. Now off you go. The car has been waiting forever,' said Grandpa, hugging the kids one final time.

Grandpa stood by the door, waving at the kids until the car turned the corner.

'Now, Dabbu, how about a nice camping trip by the river!' he said.

'Woof woof, woooooooooooo . . . oof.'

And off the two went.

A Note on the Author and the Illustrator

Stuti Agarwal is a writer, a self-proclaimed home chef and an artist. When she is not nestled in her couch, dreaming of magical adventures in her hometown of Darjeeling and one day being called Roald Dahl's prodigy, she is participating in pasta cook-offs with herself while listening to Harry Potter audiobooks and practising for the day she wins the Pulitzer.

Kavita Arvind is a design practitioner and educator. Oral histories, gender and social communication are her areas of interest. Under the banner of Chidiya Udd, she creates and teaches art, working closely with writers and publishers. She has worked with people across ages and professions and has a keen sense of how people reflect, intuit, make and learn.

About Juggernaut Kids

Juggernaut Kids is an exciting new imprint for Indian children which focuses on inspiring non-fiction, classic fiction and beautiful illustrations. We want to create great Indian stories for today's child.

Read Stuti Agarwal's Other Books

ISBN 9789386228611
80 pp
Rs 199
A/PLC

ISBN 9789386228888
192 pp
Rs 199
B/PB

To download the app scan the QR Code
with a QR scanner app